A Note to Parents and Teachers

DK READERS is a compelling program for beginning readers, designed in conjunction with leading literacy experts, including Dr. Linda Gambrell, Professor of Education at Clemson University. Dr. Gambrell has served as president of the National Reading Conference and the College Reading Association, and has recently been elected to serve as president of the International Reading Association.

Beautiful illustrations and superb full-color photographs combine with engaging, easy-to-read stories to offer a fresh approach to each subject in the series.

Each DK READER is guaranteed to capture a child's interest while developing his or her reading skills, general knowledge, and love of reading.

The five levels of DK READERS are aimed at different reading abilities, enabling you to choose the books that are exactly right for your child:

Pre-level 1: Learning to read
Level 1: Beginning to read
Level 2: Beginning to read alone
Level 3: Reading alone
Level 4: Proficient readers

The "normal" age at which a child begins to read can be anywhere from three to eight years old. Adult participation through the lower levels is very helpful in providing encouragement, discussing storylines, and sounding out unfamiliar words.

No matter which level you select, you can be sure that you are helping your child learn to read, then read to learn!

DK

LONDON, NEW YORK, MUNICH,
MELBOURNE, AND DELHI

Editor Kate Simkins
Designers Cathy Tincknell
and John Kelly
Senior Editor Catherine Saunders
Brand Manager Lisa Lanzarini
Publishing Manager Simon Beecroft
Category Publisher Alex Allan
Production Editor Siu Chan
Production Controller Amy Bennett

Reading Consultant
Linda Gambrell

First American Edition, 2008
Published in the United States by
DK Publishing
375 Hudson Street
New York, New York 10014

08 09 10 11 12 10 9 8 7 6 5 4 3 2 1

Copyright © 2008 Dorling Kindersley Limited

Published in Great Britain by Dorling Kindersley Limited.

DK books are available at special discounts for bulk purchases for
sales promotion, premiums, fund-raising, or educational use.
For details contact: DK Publishing Special Markets,
375 Hudson Street, New York, NY 10014

A Cataloging-in-Publication record for this book is available from
the Library of Congress.

ISBN 978-0-75663-849-8 (paperback)
ISBN 978-0-75663-850-4 (hardcover)

Hi-res workflow proofed by Media Development and Printing Ltd., UK.
Printed and bound in China by L-Rex Printing Co. Ltd.

Discover more at
www.dk.com

Contents

The SPY-CATCHER GANG

Written by John Kelly
Illustrated by Inklink

THE SPY~CATCHER GANG

Harry's story takes place in London in 1940. At this time, Britain was at war with Adolf Hitler's Nazi Germany. The German Army had taken control of most of western Europe and was now turning its attention to the British Isles. First, the German Air Force tried to destroy British airbases, but the Royal Air Force (RAF) fought back in an air battle called the Battle of Britain. Then, in an attack known as the Blitz, the German Air Force began dropping bombs on British cities, including London, Birmingham, Coventry, Liverpool, and Belfast. Turn to page 44 to see a map and timeline, then let the story begin....

"**My name is Harry Tucker** and I am 12 years old. I live in the East End of London with my mum and my baby sister. My dad is away fighting, and I think about him all the time. The German bombs are scary, but it is fun exploring the bombed-out buildings, even if my mum would be furious if she ever found out! I've heard that German spies could be anywhere so I am always on the lookout for them."

LONDON, 1940, NIGHT.

LIKE MOST OF LONDON, I'M TRYING TO SLEEP.

BUT I KEEP THINKING ABOUT MY DAD.

HE'S A PILOT IN THE **RAF**. I HOPE HE'S SAFE...

...BUT NO ONE'S SAFE SINCE THE WAR STARTED.

NOT EVEN IN THEIR BEDS.

WOOOOOOOOOOOOOOO

*Words in **bold** appear in the glossary on page 45.*

DID YOU KNOW? "Blitz" means "lightning" in German.

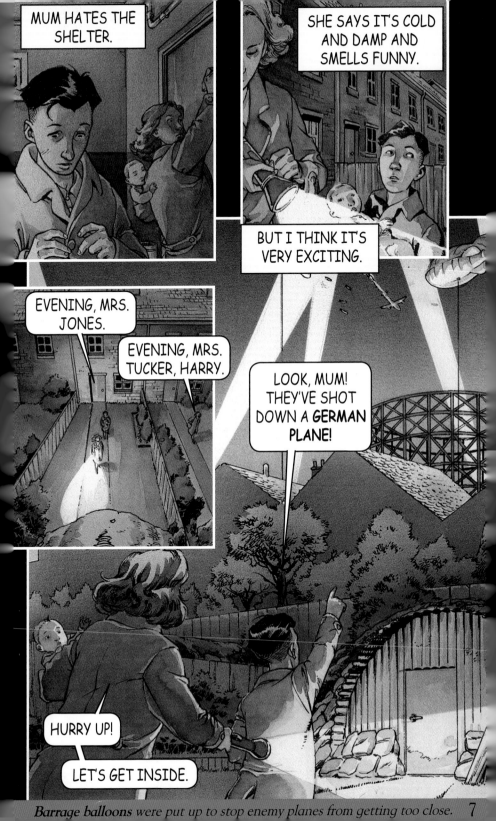

Barrage balloons were put up to stop enemy planes from getting too close. 7

I CARRY DAD'S PICTURE WITH ME EVERYWHERE.

MUM, I WISH I COULD BE A PILOT LIKE DAD AND SHOOT DOWN ENEMY PLANES.

WELL, I'M GLAD YOU'RE HERE WITH ME, DEAR.

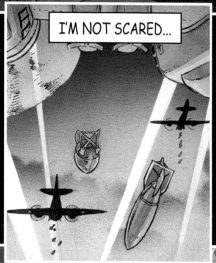

I'M NOT SCARED...

...BUT TWO BOYS FROM OUR SCHOOL WERE KILLED LAST WEEK.

IT MAKES YOU WONDER WHO WILL BE NEXT.

DID YOU KNOW? The German Air Force was called the Luftwaffe.

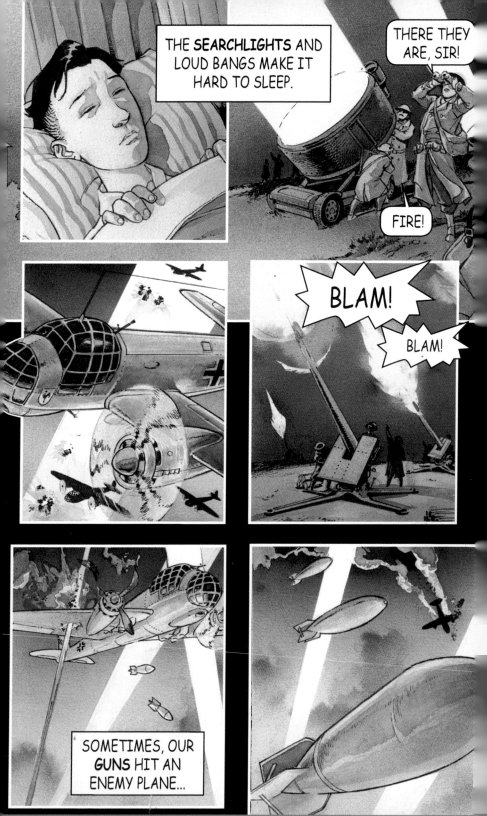

German planes bombed London for 57 nights in a row.

...BUT NOT BEFORE THEY'VE DROPPED THEIR DEADLY CARGO.

THIS IS **BBC** RADIO EARLY MORNING NEWS...

...HEAVY BOMBING OF THE **EAST END DOCKS** LAST NIGHT...

... LEFT TEN DEAD AND MANY MORE HOMELESS.

WELLINGTON STREET

DID YOU KNOW? About 20,000 people were killed in the London Blitz.

DID YOU KNOW? Many famous London buildings were damaged during the Blitz.

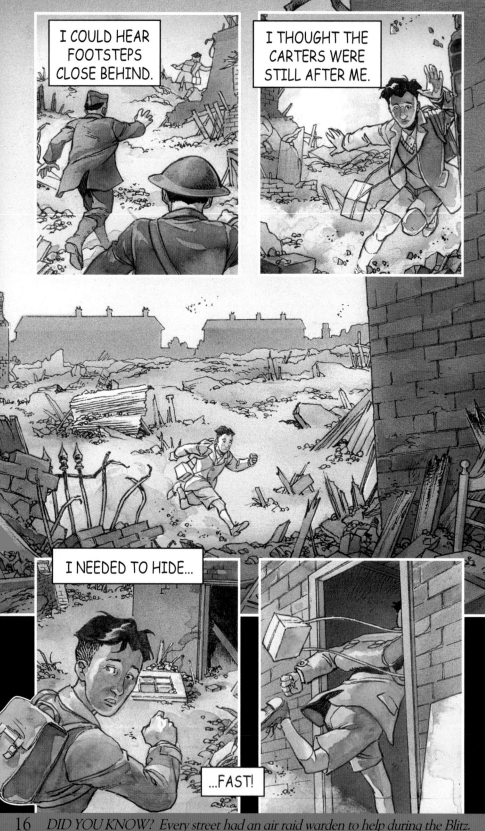

DID YOU KNOW? Every street had an air raid warden to help during the Blitz.

He or she did many important jobs, including sounding the air raid siren.

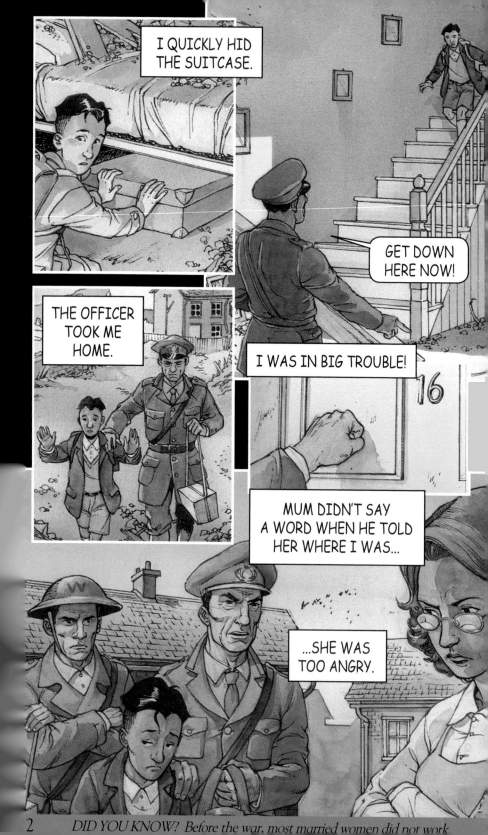

DID YOU KNOW? Before the war, most married women did not work.

DID YOU KNOW? From 1940, the British prime minister was Winston Churchill.

THE SPY'S HOUSE WAS DESERTED.

THE CASE WAS WHERE I HAD LEFT IT.

WHAT'S THAT?

SOMEONE WAS IN THE HOUSE!

OH, NO! IT MUST BE THE SPY!

He made many famous speeches to boost people's spirits and give them hope. 25

DID YOU KNOW? The worst night of the London Blitz was May 10, 1941.

About 3,000 people were killed that night.

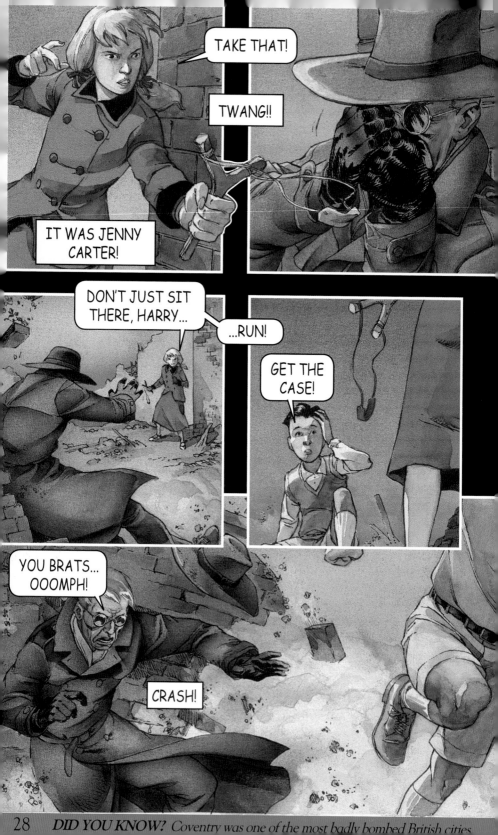

DID YOU KNOW? Coventry was one of the most badly bombed British cities

On November 14, 1940, more than 60,000 buildings were destroyed in the city. 29

DID YOU KNOW? During the Blitz, people had to cover their windows and doors

THE NEXT DAY AT SCHOOL WAS UNBEARABLE.

ALL I COULD THINK ABOUT WAS THE SPY AND HIS EVIL PLANS.

SORRY TO INTERRUPT, MISS JENKINS...

IT WAS THE DEPUTY HEADMASTER.

...I NEED TO SEE HARRY.

SNIGGER

DON'T KEEP THE HEADMASTER WAITING!

HURRY UP, BOY!

This prevented lights on the ground from guiding enemy planes.

31

DID YOU KNOW? School pupils had to practice putting on their gas masks.

I NEEDED TO WARN JENNY! I THOUGHT I KNEW WHERE THE CARTERS LIVED.

WOOOOOOOOOOOC

OH, NO! AN AIR RAID!

I HAD TO GO HOME TO THE SHELTER FIRST.

THE CASE WOULD HAVE TO WAIT.

YOU'RE HOME EARLY, DEAR!

QUICK, LET'S GET IN THE SHELTER...

...WE 'LL BE SAFE THERE!

When there was an air raid, the whole school took cover in a shelter.

DID YOU KNOW? The British government had its own shelter in London.

I HOPED THE HOUSE WOULD BE SAFE.

UP IN THE SKY...

...THE RAF WOULD FIGHT...

...TO PROTECT OUR HOMES.

THEY WOULD BEAT THE **NAZIS**.

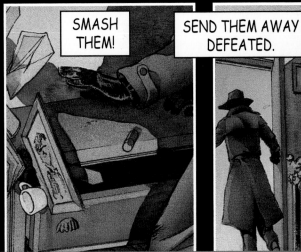

SMASH THEM!

SEND THEM AWAY DEFEATED.

The government ministers met in a bunker deep under the ground.

NOW THAT THE RAID WAS OVER, PEOPLE WERE LEAVING THE UNDERGROUND STATION.

I HAD TO FIGHT MY WAY THROUGH THE CROWDS...

...TO GET DOWN ONTO THE PLATFORMS.

JENNY! JENNY!

HARRY?

OVER HERE!

THE SPY IS AFTER ME. HE CAME TO MY SCHOOL...

DID YOU KNOW? The king and queen stayed in London during the Blitz.

DID YOU KNOW? People were told to "make do and mend" during the war.

This meant they should reuse things instead of throwing them away.

Many people celebrated on the streets of Britain.

	Queen Victoria dies		World War I	World War II		Tung takes over in China	
1901			1914–1918		1939–1945		1

1900   1920   1940

YOU ARE HERE

WORLD WAR II

There were two world wars in the 20th century. World War I (1914–1918) ended when Britain, France, the United States, and their allies (friends) defeated Germany and its allies. Germany was made to give up land and pay money to the victors. Many Germans resented this. In 1933, Adolf Hitler and his Nazi Party seized power in Germany. The Nazis promised to make Germany a strong nation once again.

World War II started in September 1939, when the German Army invaded Poland. France and Britain (the Allies) then declared war on Germany. After many fierce battles, the Germans took control of most of western Europe. Hitler then prepared to invade the British Isles. In 1940, the German Air Force began bombing British cities in an attempt to make Britain surrender.

Germany attacked Russia in 1941, so the Russians joined the war on the side of the Allies. Germany, Italy, and Japan formed an alliance (the Axis). In 1941, Japan bombed US ships in Pearl Harbor, Hawaii, bringing the US into the war. Soon, there was fighting all over the globe. The war in Europe ended when Allied troops invaded Germany in May 1945. Japan surrendered in August 1945.

Neutral states

Axis states

Areas controlled by Axis

Allied states

Areas controlled by Allies

Extent of German military occupation

A map of Europe in 1942. Most of Europe and some of North Africa were occupied by Axis troops.

Mount Everest
climbed for
first time
'53

1969
land on
the Moon

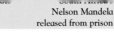Nelson Mandela
released from prison
1990

TIMELIN

1960   1980   2000

GLOSSARY

LONDON   PAGE 5

London is a city in southern England and is the capital of the United Kingdom.

RAF   PAGE 5

"RAF" stands for the "Royal Air Force," which is the British Air Force. In World War II, RAF planes defended the skies over Britain from German planes and also dropped bombs on enemy cities.

AIR RAID SIRENS   PAGE 6

Air raid sirens were machines that made a loud wailing noise—loud enough to wake people up if they were asleep. The sirens told people that there were enemy planes on the way and that they should go to a shelter.

SHELTER   PAGE 6

An air raid shelter was a place that people could go where they would be safe from the bombs. Many people had "Anderson shelters" in their backyards. These temporary shelters were made of curved panels of steel that joined together to form the roof and sides. Some people had small steel shelters in their homes and others sheltered in London Underground subway stations.

BOMBED   PAGE 6

German planes started dropping bombs (metal cases full of explosives) on London on September 7, 1940. They bombed the city almost every night or day until May 10, 1941.

GERMAN PLANE   PAGE 7

The German planes that dropped bombs on British cities were mainly a type called Heinkel bombers.

BARRAGE BALLOONS   PAGE 7

These large balloons were attached to the ground by steel cables. They were designed to prevent enemy planes from getting too close to the ground.

SEARCHLIGHTS — PAGE 9

From the ground, British soldiers shined beams of light from huge lamps called searchlights onto German planes. This made the planes easier for the soldiers to see and shoot at.

GUNS — PAGE 9

Antiaircraft guns on the ground fired at enemy planes.

BBC — PAGE 10

"BBC" stands for the "British Broadcasting Corporation." During World War II, most people listened to the BBC radio for news about the war. The BBC also made television programs, but few people had television sets at this time.

EAST END DOCKS — PAGE 10

The large area in the east of London is commonly known as the East End. During World War II, the East End docks (where ships were loaded and unloaded) were often the targets of bombing raids. Most people living in the East End during the war were fairly poor and worked in factories or at the docks. Because family and friends all lived in the same area, people could look after each other during the terrible times of the Blitz.

SHRAPNEL — PAGE 11

Pieces of metal thrown out by a bomb when it explodes.

BOMB SITES — PAGE 11

Places where bombs have exploded and destroyed the buildings.

GAS MASK   PAGE 12

A gas mask is worn over the face to stop the wearer from breathing in

 poisonous gas. During World War II, every person in Britain had to carry a gas mask to protect him or her from poison gas attacks by the Germans, although there were actually no gas attacks in World War II.

EVACUATED   PAGE 14

Sent away from a place of danger.

IDENTITY CARDS   PAGE 19

When the war started in 1939, the British government decided that everyone should carry identity cards. The cards had information about each person, including his or her name and address.

RATION BOOKS   PAGE 19

During the war, ships bringing things such as food and clothes to Britain were attacked. This meant that many things started to run out, so to make sure everyone got a fair share, the government gave every family a ration book. Each book contained coupons that people could use in stores in exchange for clothes and essential foods such as butter, milk, eggs, sugar, and meat.

BOMB DISPOSAL OFFICER   PAGE 20

Any bombs that did not explode when they hit the ground had to be made safe. This was the job of the bomb disposal officers, who were specially trained soldiers.

DEFUSING   PAGE 20

Bombs contain fuses—switches that make the bomb explode. The fuse has to be removed to make the bomb safe. This is called defusing.

SPY PAGE 23

A spy is someone who finds out secret information. During World War II, the British government warned people not to talk to strangers in case they were German spies and to be careful what they said in public.

DETECTIVE SERGEANT PAGE 32

A detective sergeant is a British police officer who tries to solve major crimes. He does not wear a uniform.

NAZIS PAGE 35

The Nazis were a group of people, led by Adolf Hitler, who ruled Germany from 1933 to 1945. They believed that the Germans were better than any other race and that many of Gemany's problems were caused by Jews.

LOOTERS PAGE 36

Looters are people who steal from houses and stores in wartime or during riots.

UNDERGROUND PAGE 37

The railroad that travels beneath London's streets is called the Underground or the tube. During the war, people took shelter on the subway station platforms and often stayed there all night.

RUBBLE PAGE 40

Piles of broken pieces from buildings that have been blown up.

GAS LEAK PAGE 40

Gas is a fuel that is used mainly for cooking and heating. It is invisible but easily set on fire, and if any gas escapes from a pipe, it may cause an explosion.

SPIV PAGE 41

Spivs were people who stole rationed goods and sold them to people at high prices, especially during and just after World War II. This was against the law, but many people bought from spivs because they couldn't get what they needed any other way. The buying and selling of illegal goods is called the black market.

GAS LINE PAGE 42

A gas line is a large pipe that carries gas to a street of houses.